Clint Faraday
book forty three
Dead Aunts

Clint is visiting friends in Culantro on his way to Quebrada Tula when Rigo, a student at the university, says his only problem lately is dead aunts. He is practicing English. Clint asks what could be the problem with dead ants? Sweep them out.

"What killed them? Poison?"

Juan says they were all strangled.

"How do you strangle and ant?" Clint asked, then added, "Oh, shit!"

Clint Faraday
book forty three
Dead Aunts
© 2019 by C. D. Moulton

all rights reserved: no part of this publication may be reproduced or transmitted in any form or by any means, electronic or mechanical, including photocopy, recording, or any other information retrieval system, without permission in writing from the copyright holder/ publisher, except in the case of brief quotations embodied in critical articles or reviews.

This is a work of fiction. Any resemblances to persons, living or dead, or events is purely coincidental unless otherwise stated.

Contents

About the author

CD Moulton has traveled extensively over much of the world both in the music business, where he was a rock guitarist, songwriter and arranger and in an import/export business. He has been everything from a bar owner to auto salvage (junkyard) manager, longshoreman to high steel worker, orchid grower to landscaper, tropical fish farmer to commercial fisherman. He started writing books in 1983 and has published more than 350 books as of January 1, 2023. His most popular books to date are about research with orchids, though much of his science fiction and fantasy work has proven popular. He wrote the CD Grimes, PI series, and the Det. Nick Storie series, Clint Faraday series, and many other works.

He now resides in Gualaca, Chiriqui, Panamá, where he writes books, plays music with friends, does research with orchids and medicinal plants. He has lately become involved in fighting for the rights of the indigenous people, who are among his closest friends, and in fighting the extreme corruption in the courts and police in Panamá.

He offers the free e-book, *Fading Paradise*, that explains what he has been through because of the corruption.

CD is the discoverer of the Chadam Protocol for curing cancer.

Facebook page Ambrosia peruviana for cancer.

"Well, we certainly can't say we're getting tired of Cusapín!" Clint Faraday, retired PI from Florida, now declared a Ngobe Indio, much to his great pride, said to his beautiful Ngobe wife. "I thought we'd be there for five or six months and it was more than a year! I'm in better physical shape than I've ever been in my life!"

"Yeah, Dad! I could stay there forever!" Clint's almost seven year old son said. "I wish they had as good a school there as on Isla San Cristobal."

"Clint's building a school there," Tyna, his wife, said. "It's more a problem of finding good teachers among the Ngobe."

"They're good teachers!" Nicole, their five year old daughter, insisted. "They just don't teach the same things. The council won't let them bring in all that religious crap so they can't get a lot of what they need."

"The teachers got their education with all that propaganda," Tyna agreed. "The churches supply most of the teaching material. We don't need their god with our education."

"I'm going to look for teachers before we go to

Tula," Clint promised. "Judi (Judi Lum, their attractive Oriental neighbor in Bocas Town on Isla Colón) considers that part of her duties in the corporation, but she's taken on a hell of a lot more than any one person should have on her shoulders. Manny's looking for good teachers, too. He says the good ones are mostly already working. We'll have to find them as they're graduated from the better universities. We're sponsoring forty two of them now, but it'll be next year before any of them get their degrees."

"Well, we're going to find a place for Nito to stay while he's in school where there's already a good teacher," Tyna said. "Juanito's son, Rigo, is getting his degree in six more months and will go to Quebrada Tula to the school you built there. He's supposed to be good. Manny said he's a lot better than anything the regular classes usually graduate. Nito will only have to stay in Soloy for six months. It should work out pretty well."

They put all their belongings into the truck/taxi and Clint instructed the driver to take them to Boca del Morito. A friend would be there to take them on to Soloy. He was going to visit Juanito Morales and his family and several other friends in Culantro, have a conversation with Rigo about the school, then go on to Soloy the next day. He had old friends he wanted to spend some time with there. He would leave his car with them and would take the bus to Soloy.

He arrived in Culantro in the afternoon and went to a pensión. Several would insist he stay with them, but he could say he had business to handle – which was very true! The school – and needed to stay in town. None of them lived very close to the center.

He went to Gala's Restaurant for a good pollo guisadas dinner and talked with Andres and Yahaira a bit there, then went to the China for a few personal things, then out to the cantina. He learned Juanito hadn't been in town for about a week. Rigo was at the university at night and would be home about eleven. He could see him in the morning.

He talked with most of the people he knew there, then went to the pensión to sack out. He called Tyna and talked for half an hour before going to bed.

In the morning he talked with the people in the restaurant and met a couple new friends, then drove out the rough road to where Juanito had his finca. Marta was fixing Rigo breakfast and he joined them. Juanito had gone to milk the cows and would be back in an hour or so.

"Well! You're doing pretty good in the school, I hear!" Clint said to Rigo, in English. Rigo was taking courses and wanted to learn. He would speak English except to his mother. They would use the Indio dialect of the area. She would speak to Clint in Spanish because he didn't know much of the local dialect. They would all learn.

They chatted about things, then Clint said he wanted to know how things were going. Any problems in school?

"No. It is easy for me. I will go to Quebrada Tula to administer the school you are building. I can teach some all the basics they will to need (Clint corrected him, as agreed, about not using the "to" before the verb in the infinitive form). Yes. Need *to* go *to* university *to* obtain a degree *to* teach."

"Everything else is okay? Do you need funds for anything?"

"All is well except the problem with the dead aunts."

"I don't understand? Tyna just sweeps them out if she has to get rid of them. Were they poisoned? I can't see a problem."

"Sweep them...? Now I don't understand. They were strangled, not poisoned."

"Strangled? How in hell do you strangle an ant?

"Oh, shit!"

"What?"

"In English 'ant' and 'aunt' are almost the same word – in sound. I thought you meant armigas!

You were talking about tias. What happened?"

He smiled. "I will have to remember about ho-mo-phones. That word is too like ho-mo-phobes.

"They were at their big house on the finca. Abuela left them that half and abuelo left this place to Papa. Aunt Luisa has the boy and girl that mother is taking care of now. They left very early for the school. Aunt Magali has the girl. She is old enough to stay on the finca. Aunt Nilsa doesn't have any children. I think Don Carlos Flores wants to buy the finca, but they would not sell it.

"He's the caballero with the very big finca close to the coast. His land is to the west of the finca.

"Six days ago on Wednesday morning, Luisa was found in the barn with a wire twisted around her neck. Milio helps her with the milking. He brings the cows to her. He found her.

"Wednesday night Aunt Nilsa went down to the river to turn the water tank off. It was full. It's the one that she uses for her vegetables garden. She didn't ever go back to the house and Aunt Magali went to find her because Aunt Luisa had been strangled. She took her gun, but Aunt Nilsa was in the water with a wire twisted around her neck.

"Aunt Magali made the arrangements for Aunt Luisa's children with Mama. She kept the gun close and stayed in the house. She didn't know what was happening and was frightened.

"Sunday morning Magalita found Aunt Magali strangled in the kitchen.

"The police are investigating. I don't think they will discover anything. They are not very good. I know they are all dishonest because Magalita's novio is one. He is a mestizo and he is stupid about our ways. He is a ladron. He brags about making gringos pay him or he will take them in for identification questions."

"You can report that! President Martinelli's cracked down on that kind of thing!"

"We have to report to Captain Ramón. He is as bad. Nothing happens except that the one who reported has an ID check every time he goes to town."

"Maybe I'll do a little checking and reporting of my own! This gringo can pull a few little stunts on his own!"

"Tell me everything you know about the deaths of your aunts."

"There is not much I can tell you. I only know they were strangled with the wire twisted around their necks."

Clint thought for a minute. He was going to see what he could see about this situation. He had caused police officers who discriminated against the Indios no end of trouble before. He wasn't the least adverse to doing it again.

"Do you have a map of the area where you can show me how to get to the aunts' finca?"

Rigo found a plano layout that showed that all the land to the west of the finca, including the peninsula, was owned by the man who wanted to buy the finca. He would then own all the land surrounding the town except the national land to the east and to the coast there.

They talked for awhile, then Rigo went on to the university. Juanito came in and greeted Clint. They sat for a cup of hot coffee. Juanito couldn't add anything about his sister's deaths. Clint promised to investigate.

"You will not have cooperation with the police here," Juanito warned. "They are ladrones."

"I know how to deal with corrupt ladrones," Clint replied. "Maybe they'll learn a little something about intimidation."

He soon headed back to Culantro. He parked outside of Gala's and went in to see what the gossip was about the dead women. There was none. No one mentioned them and would change the subject if Clint did. When he went back out a police officer demanded his ID. He smirked to himself and handed the cop his cedula.

"This isn't in order! You will come with me to have it checked with the main offices! You will show me your passport! Now!"

"Okay. I have some business with the police department here. My wife has my passport with her in Soloy, though I don't have to have one."

"Well, there is a fifty dollar fine for not having your passport!"

"No there isn't. I think you'd better take a closer look at the carnet. It's a cedula, not a residency or tourist card.

"Maybe I should have shown you this." He handed him the card that stated he was an official investigative expert working with the Policía Nacional. "Shall we go to the station? I have a few questions that *you* will answer. Now!"

Clint marched with the officer, R. Martinez, to the station. Martinez kept trying to explain that he was only following orders about strangers in town because there had recently been trouble from strangers.

"So you pull an act about improper ID when there was no such thing. It's a very old way to shake down people. You'd be wise to shut the hell up! All you're doing is making things worse for yourself Martinelli says an automatic four years for corrupt cops!"

He didn't shut up. He was as much as whining by the time they got to the station. The corregidor was close and there were a lot of people standing around outside of the office. Mostly Indios.

Clint went to talk with several of them. They were all being shaken down. They didn't have much and those ladrones were taking what little they had or they would go to jail. Clint stormed into the office and demanded they shut down. Immediately! They were to leave the office, lock it, and give him the keys. Anyone who went back inside until he said they could would be held and incarcerated for one year.

He didn't have the authority to do that, but they didn't know it. He watched to see no one took anything out other than their personal items. He called Panamá City and explained what he had done to the new head man, Randolfo Hernandez. He had worked with him before in Bocas and in David. He explained what he had found and done. Dolfo gave him authority and would send some people he could trust from David. He faxed orders to the police station that Clinton Faraday, Specialist, was fully in charge. The station's offices were to be closed and locked. Nothing was to be removed. There would be an inquiry by the Junta Nacionál de Frente de Corrupcion. Any evidence of corruption or bribery would result in an automatic minimum sentence of four years in prison, as per orders of President Martinelli.

Clint met Capitan Felix Ramón. He was not impressed. Ramón was overweight and had an attitude. He was just short of threatening, but Clint said threatening him would prove most inadvisable just before he crossed the line. He stomped out.

What a great way to start a multiple murder investigation! Alienate the cops.

On the other hand, they rather apparently weren't doing any investigating.

A young woman came running into the station as they were locking it up and demanded to speak with Officer Ricardo Martinez. He was her novio.

"You are Magalita Lopez?" Clint asked.

"Yes. What is this?"

"Your boyfriend was shaking the people down. That's against the law. He'll get four years for it. Anything else?"

"It's all lies! He was not! They're lying!"

"He tried to shake me down. It wasn't from complaints from others. That corregidor is in it up to his neck!"

"The corregidor's in the hospital in David. It's his assistant who's running the office. I know he is evil, but there's nothing we can do about it. The corregidor, the real one, doesn't know what they're doing. Jutieres has been in the hospital for almost two years.

"I don't believe Ricardo was trying to, as you said, shake you down. You misunderstood him. Maybe that capitan would, but not my Ricardo."

"Wake up! They were damned well shaking down our people! Don't try to defend them!"

"*Our* people? You are not ... then you are Clint Faraday, Ngobe by council declaration?"

"The same."

"I swear to you that I didn't know Ricardo was a part of that. He was only doing what he was ordered to do by the jefe."

"I ... okay. I'll accept that, until proven different. If people are going to testify against him he's gone!"

Ramón went by in the police truck. Ricardo was with him. Two officers were in back. The one who said he was the corregidor was in the back with the cops.

"What's that one's name?" Clint asked. "The one who told me he was the corregidor?"

"Him? Beto Jimenez. He's a ladron."

Clint grinned and made a quick phone call. That police truck wasn't going far.

Now. Wait until the new crew from David got there at Gala's. He wanted to see what evidence was in the station about what he now considered his case. Dead aunts.

He went around town to find what he could about the legal corregidor. It seemed he was in office only a few weeks and had some kind of health problem that left him incapable of running the office. He had let Ramón select the acting assistant. The real assistant was Pablo Diniro, who Ramón said was much too young and inexperienced to hold the office. Why the real secretary, A Srta. Mostas, was gone, no one knew.

After about two hours the police truck with four officers came to the station. Esteban Valdez and

Celio Angel were the heads of the units until others with experience could be brought from Panamá City. Julia Gortas and Fedrico Manchos were the two others. Valdez said he was to take orders from Clint until further notice.

"No way! You're in charge! The only order I give is that you enforce the law and don't try to shake anyone down. There are no gringos or mestizos or blacks or Indios here, only people. Clear?"

"Very. You will work with us? You will gather evidence from the corregidor's office and from the capitan's office?"

"Of course." Clint introduced the new police to the people he knew and asked that they cooperate with each other. Things were going to change.

He went with Valdez to the corregidor's office. A woman jumped out of the back window when they came into the front. Julia and Celio were back there. They'd bring her in through the front door.

She had been doing something with the files in the corregidor's consulting room. The drawers were open and papers were strewn around the room. The computer was on, but she hadn't done anything on it yet. She was probably going to erase it.

Julia brought Amanda Bertos Verde in carrying

a large plastic bag of files. She had been the acting secretary. She started screaming about unauthorized persons going into the corregidor's files. She would have the president himself bring charges for that!

Clint handed her his papers stating he was a specialist and was in charge. She started whining that Ramón and Jimenez made her do it! She was just a woman who worked in an office until they came! She didn't know what Jimenez was until he was already there and she couldn't do anything about it. She thought he was a good man is why she had recommended him and she wanted a lawyer and, oh God! How did she get involved in this?! She didn't know anything and she was in the middle of it and why did everyone want her advice, then turn on her?

"Why do all you sleazeball crooks *whine* when you're caught?" Clint asked. "It was *your* game. You played and lost, then you *whine*?

"Lt. Gortas, put her in the jail with everyone not there for a violent crime – and let the ones who are there for non-violent crimes go. Tell them we'll investigate and will purge their records. All funds we can recover from those involved will be returned to the victims of their corruption."

She saluted and started out with Bertos, who decided she would refuse to move. Gortas drug her out.

"She doesn't take any bullshit, does she?" Clint asked, grinning.

"Julia? Not much," Valdez answered.

They went through the files still there and Clint called Rigo, who would come with two other students he could trust and would straighten out the office.

He went over to the records computer and went through the files. It had all the cases listed as to subject, date, time and resolution. There were hundreds of twenty to fifty dollar fines. There were nine people in jail for non-payment. There were only two legitimate cases in more than a month of such phony trials.

They went back to the station, leaving Celio there to guard and to work with Rigo and his friends when they arrived.

Clint couldn't find anything about the dead aunts except that they were dead of strangulation and where and when the bodies were discovered. There was no investigation at the scenes.

Clint sat back to think. It had to come down to crooked cops. Did they, or one of them, commit the three murders or were they only paid not to investigate? What was it about?

That automatically put Ricardo Martinez smack in the middle of it. Was Magalita part of it or was she the innocent she seemed?

Clint damned well intended to find out!

He would first talk with a lot of the local people about the women and about the police in general. How were they able to keep this travesty from being reported?

Clint went to Gala's, where he talked with a lot of people. They seemed to think that was the way it always was. The ones from even a short distance from the town didn't seem to know anything like that was going on.

Rigo came in in the afternoon to introduce Lilia Gomez, Sylvia Natchez and Salvatore Emedes. They were all in their final semester and had gone through the university with him.

Clint took him aside and asked why no one had reported the crooked police. He said he'd only heard a few stories and figured it was guys who got drunk and into trouble. The police had only stopped him one time. "Ricardo was one of the officers close and had come to say he knew me and that I was a top student at university and wouldn't be stupid enough to be on the streets without proper identification."

"No one told you what they were doing?"

"Other than the things police always do, no. Everyone knows they will cause you trouble if you don't maybe give them a dollar for a soda now and then.”

“They *don't* always do that. Not since the crackdown, although most of that’s in Panamá City. Martinelli doesn’t seem to concentrate anywhere else.

“I just thought of something. How long has the crew we caught been here? Ricardo and Ramón and accomplices?”

“Well, Ramón was here for ... years. Since Gregorio died. Ricardo, about a year and a half or more.”

“I see. Now we have to find why they weren’t rotated. This could get a lot bigger than a few crooked cops in a little town.”

Valdez came to ask what the students were to do. Clint told him they were to carefully go through the files at the corregidor’s office and list the dates and times and resolution of all cases and put the files back in order.

“Esteban, how long have you been in your present station?”

“How long? Four months. We’re rotated every six months ... I see! How long has this crew been here?”

“Years. Even the beat cops, like Ricardo, have been here more than a year.”

“So. We have to find who allowed that.”

“Minimum. We have to find how many little

towns have the same situation and who's getting a cut. It's going to get dangerous."

"The truck was stopped, or found by the road about four kilometers toward the carretera. No one was about. They have had several hours to get away. It is obvious they have somewhere to go."

"It's also as obvious they haven't considered that they're now a deadly danger to someone. We have to learn how many places there are that are doing this. Quietly. Maybe just some stranger going through town to visit friends or relatives?"

Valdez nodded and looked grim. He said he had to get word to people in the capital without anyone here knowing. Clint said he would arrange that.

The small radio Valdez was carrying made a loud attention call. He answered and was told the bodies of Beto Jimenez and Felix Ramón were found killed execution-style by a little creek seven kilometers toward Chiriqui.

"Were there any others?" Clint asked.

"Not there. A Srta. Serena Mostas and a Pablo Diniro were found on the road to Las Lajas, but they were killed with strangulation. With a wire twisted around their necks. We don't know if the killings are connected at this point, though those people were from that area and worked with the police and corregidor."

"They're connected," Clint said. "That will be all of them except Ricardo, which means he's the mole and that he killed the aunts. Try to find him. He's the big quarry that can lead us to the top man."

"So. He was in charge here. They pretended that Ramón was so no one would look at him. I think that is how it will be?"

"Likely. He'd be dead if it was the other way around.

"I think I'd heard the names. Pablo Diniro and Mostas."

"Diniro was assistant to the actual corregidor. Serena Mostas was the secretary."

"So. They knew too much, now that it's hit the fan, so had to go."

"Hit the fan...? What does that mean ... oh. It hits the fan and is blown out for all to see?"

"Something like that."

"Clint, there is something very sinister behind this mess. People are still very much afraid, even with us having their oppressors removed."

"That means the real oppressor isn't removed."

Valdez bit his lip and nodded.

Clint got a lot of papers and put them in his car. He was just leaving when Rigo called to say they had found something strange. A ledger in the corregidor's personal office hidden behind the files. It was labeled "Don Muerte" and seemed to be a list of sums of money and dates.

"_Don_ Muerte? Could it be _Doc_ Muerte?"

"I don't think so. Maybe ... oh. Dr. Death. I see. Maybe that is how it was meant to be read, Don instead of Doc in case someone found it. Don Muerte means Mr. Death. It could be that, too."

Clint agreed. Now he would have to find out who Mr. Death was. It could be the real head honcho.

He drove out and to Horconcitos where he left his car and used a police car to go to David, where he explained the whole case to the police and had all his papers faxed to Policía Nacionál in Panamá City. There would be a check with national headquarters of just who wasn't being rotated on schedule. There were a few places where officers stayed at the request of the public. Any other would be discreetly checked out.

Clint then went back to Horconcitos for his car, then back to Culantro.

Esteban showed him the ledger. It was a typical form that's sold in office supply stores with a big "Ledger" diagonally across the front. The pages were standard columns that were labeled 1– 2 – 3 and 4, then TTL. The first was the standard date form that started with 6/3/2011 and ended with four days ago, 28/7/2012. There were entries on an average of twice a week. Columns 1 and 2 started from the first. 3 started 14/9/2011 and 4 started 1/2/2012.

Clint looked at the dates and raised an eyebrow at Valdez.

"It started when R. Martinez came to work. Three is when Jorge Samosa came to work. Four is when Carla Renceres came to work."

The amounts ranged from a low of Bl/3.60 to a high of Bl/84.80.

Clint checked 26/12/2011. There were entries in columns 1 and 2. Bl/21.25 and Bl/18.40. The TTL column had Bl/23.80?

He checked 16/5/2012, his birthday. 1 = 4.50, 2 = 21.00, 3 = 9.20, 4 = 6.40. That made a total of 41.10. The TTL column had Bl/24.50.

"I'd say Mr. Death receives a little more than half," Valdez said.

Clint divided the TTL by the full amount in both. "Sixty percent."

"About three thousand a year."

Clint nodded. "We have to find out who Mr. Death is. The people in this one little town were being robbed of about five grand a year. If he has this going on in other places, he's going to answer to those people. The Policía Nacionál will be occupied with a demonstration out on the main highway at the time."

Valdez looked grim and nodded.

"How long until we get the reports about other places?" Clint asked.

"Probably as they're found. All of them within twenty four hours."

"I'll move around. Something occurred to me about the way people act. They wouldn't discuss any of this with anyone. Mr. Death will be here. Close. I want to see how people react when the hoity-toits come to town."

"Maybe they don't know which one it is. Maybe they're afraid to say anything bad about anybody because of that."

Clint had to agree, but he remembered something. It was just possible there was someone ... he knew who it almost had to be! It was going to be hell to prove, but he was sure he knew what the dead aunts were about.

"Esteban, I want to know the entire personal records on those four crooked cops. I want to see the connection. I want all you can find about Beto Jimenez. He has to figure into it. He was put there. He didn't just happen to fall into the job. This ledger started with Martinez. When did Jimenez get into the picture?"

"When Jutieres went to the hospital. The same time Martinez joined ... I wonder if he ever went through police training. It is too possible he is not ever a legal police officer."

"That's part of what I want to know from their personal records.

"What happened that put the corregidor – you said Jutieres? – in the hospital?"

Valdez spent some time going through papers. He shook his head and called the hospital in David. They would report whatever was legal and pertinent directly to Dolfo, who would call within the hour.

Clint and Valdez found the personnel files and studied them. Martinez had some credits listed as a security guard with minimal training. There was no way he was a legal Policía Nacionál officer. Ramón had the police training, was average in performance, had been a street patrol officer in Penonomé as his only duty before coming to Culantro by request of the citizens.

"That culebra was brought here by the citizens? Bullshit!" Clint snarled.

"He will have a close relative here. A powerful relative. I would say a relative who goes by the name of Don Muerte!" Valdez replied.

"We have to find who."

Valdez read over each sheet very carefully, then passed it to Clint. The previous history of Felix Ramón stated he was born near Las Palmas, Veraguas. That was close. His mother was Anita Salderos C. and his father was unknown.

"Maybe Mr. Death is the father?" Valdez said. Clint shrugged. "His schooling was paid for with an anonymous grant. It's entirely too possible.

"Esteban, I'm using my detective training in identifying disguised people and just thought of something.

"What do you have on Martinez?"

"Very little. He was born ... here. His mother is Gilda Hernandez. Father is suspected to have been Arturo Veladero. I have met this Gilda Hernandez. She has Alzheimer's and won't be able to give any information."

The radio signal buzzed and Valdez answered. It was Dolfo.

"Clint? Bino Jutieres had some kind of stroke or something. He's a vegetable now. The way they worded this makes me think he was poisoned, like too many. It wasn't quite enough to kill him, just enough to kill his mind. Do you know what thallium is? Traces were found in him that they couldn't purge."

"I know what it is. Don Muerte is really in for it with me now! I'll feed him just enough that he'll be a vegetable with a mind that feels pain and a body that doesn't work!"

"Who in hell is Don Muerte?"

"We're trying to find that information now," Valdez answered. "All I can say is that he makes a fer de lance a preferred companion!"

They exchanged what little information they had and signed off. Clint sat back to think.

Dolfo called back. "Clint, this is just coming in. About the non-rotated police officers.

"We've now found two other places with a like situation. None of what we have is close to you. It's probably not connected. We moved in suddenly and have locked them down. These are not going to take any truck to try to escape.

"I think your situation there is isolated."

"Thanks, Dolfo. This is one sick mess. I think we have a closet sadist, personally. He wants to take over the area and run it his way. He's Count Dracula without the vampire shit. He's going to be someone who's very proper and generous and liked – on the surface."

"Take the very greatest care, my friend. Those people are doubly dangerous when you don't know who they are."

"That, you can bet the farm on!"

They soon signed off. Clint said he was going to move around town to try to get some answers.

"You won't get any answers if this goes as it has been going."

"I have a method I was taught by a neighbor in Bocas. I'm a tenth as good at it as she is, but it does work. It's based on getting answers to the questions you don't ask."

Valdez gave him a funny look.

Clint went to Gala's and ordered the comida corriente, a pork chop, rice, frijoles and a mixed salad and banana fried in honey. It cost $2.00.

He spoke with several people in the restaurant about the crooked corregidor. Most people didn't know what had happened to the real assistant and secretary. They became very wary when Clint told them how they were killed. He said Martinez was the only one not dead. He had to be the one who killed them.

No response except glances at each other and a little feeling of fear showing in their eyes and manner. He changed the subject. He didn't want to endanger anyone more than they already were simply because they lived here.

He saw Magalita, but decided to wait to talk to her until he had a few more facts together. The way this stood at the moment he didn't have all the questions he wanted to ask.

He went to the corregidor's office to talk for an hour or more with Rigo and the students. They didn't have too hard a time with the records, but Rigo reported there were large gaps, particularly when gringos were brought in and no resolution was listed on any of their cases. They could, therefore, safely assume that the gringos paid off the corregidor.

"We checked the phone numbers called. They are listed automatically. No one had erased the record. We did not call them. I feel you will want to do that." He handed Clint a long list, four pages, of numbers dialed and numbers received. Clint read quickly down the lists and noted that a good many were to a name, not a number. That would mean they were entered for speed dial.

"DM" called every Saturday at 2:00 sharp. That would be Don Muerte. Clint started to call the number to see who answered, then stopped. It would be just plain stupid to call from that phone. The number would show up on DM's caller ID and would alert DM to get rid of that phone. It was a celular number.

He took out his own phone, put it on "hide ID"

and punched the number. It rang three times, then, "Habla."

"Wha...! Er, is Dona there?"

"There is no Dona here," a cultured voice replied. "You have the wrong number."

"Seis seis ocho quatro nueve dos cero uno?"

"No. Nueve dos uno cero."

"Desculpame. Mi falta!" he rang off. He had hoped the caller would give his name, but Clint was sure he knew it.

He took the list to the station, where he checked out several numbers who called regularly. They seemed legitimate.

Valdez came in to ask if Clint was making any progress. Clint said he had to see a few people. He thought part of it was solved.

"You will call them from that list. I see."

"No. I meant it literally. I have to see them."

That got another funny look.

Clint went into town to get a look at the people there who might be part, if unknowingly, of this sordid mess. He had spotted something that could prove damned important.

Gilda Hernandez didn't have the feature he was looking for. That was encouraging. It could only be dominant in males. That meant the strange shape of the ears was probably only from Ricardo's father's side.

Gilda was almost a mental blank. She was living at a sister's place. Clint told the sister, Manda, he knew it was a strange request, but it had to do with a police investigation. Did she have any pictures of Arturo Veladero?

She had several. The feature was not on his ears. He was more certain than ever he was on the right track. He now had to find the father of at least two of the crooked cops. He was looking at what he was sure was a dominant trait in the males in that family.

His prime suspect didn't live in Culantro. He was closer to the coast. How would Clint be able to meet him?

He asked around and found that there was a town called Remedios, which he knew, where it was likely he would go for entertainment. There was nothing in Culantro to hold a rich person's attention. It was Friday so was a likely time for him to go out.

He went back to the corregidor's office. Rigo and the students had just finished and Rigo had an outline to show what they had done. He asked if he knew his suspect, but Rigo had seen him around at times, but had never spoken to him. He didn't consort with the local commoners. That solidified Clint's ideas a bit more.

It was five twenty. He could clean up and dress and head for Remedios. He could be there about eight or eight thirty. He could manage to run into his suspect – if he was there.

Clint went into the combination bar-brothel-restaurant-hotel and looked over the situation. It sounded like a dump when he heard about it and lived down to expectations. The selection wasn't much, but he wasn't interested in that. No one in Panamá could hold a candle to his wife.

The food was very good there, at least. He had lasagna, which a few places in David made, but he couldn't think of another where it was as good as this. Maybe Mi Bacata.

He used the technique Judi had taught him to gather information. It resulted in his finding his suspect came in regularly on both Saturday and Sunday nights. He learned that by saying he was staying in Culantro and there wasn't anything to do there at night. He was told that one person from Culantro or close came in. Was he the one who recommended the place?

Clint said that he might have been. He didn't remember who it was. This is very good lasagna!

He went back to Juanito's early. He would stay around town Saturday and go back to Remedios at about the same time. He would make a better plan of how he would act and what he would say. It had to be flexible to a great extent. He would be dealing with a personality type that had a wide variation in its responses.

He also had to find a way to connect anyone not already known to anything. He did think he had a fairly good lever. He also had to hope his quarry had a strange configuration of the ears. If not, he could be wrong all along.

He did think of one thing that had to be checked out. He asked Valdez to find out what he could about the police in Remedios. It wouldn't be a very good idea to depend on them if they were letting Ramón and company slide on anything. That would put them in the pocket of the wrong people!

"They had a complaint filed by a gringo named Smith against the police and corregidor about three months ago. He claimed they had shaken him down for two hundred fifty dollars. Capitan Ramón and Corregidor Jimenez had sent the case papers to them. Smith was driving with illegal alcohol content. He was let off easy because he was a tourist and would suffer everywhere he went with that charge against his driver's license. They made it a charge of reckless driving instead and fined him for that instead of the one thousand two hundred dollars for drunk drivers. Now he was claiming they shook him down? It was the other way around!

"That's about it from Remedios. There's a good crew there."

"So they had it set up to where the police and corregidor would protect each other."

"It certainly appears that such was the case!"

Not much else happened then. He talked with Juanito and Marta about Ricardo Martinez. They didn't know much about him except that they thought he was a thief and they didn't like or trust him.

"Did he ever talk about any place he knew other than here?"

Marta said he had once talked about catching a

big tuna near Hicaco. His cousin has a fishing boat there.

Clint looked up Hicaco. It was out near Santa Catalina, Veraguas.

He changed his plans a little about who he was going to confront first. He put some beach things together and drove to Hicaco, getting there just after dark. He found a pensión and checked in, then went to a little local food restaurant that had surprisingly good pescado. He didn't ask, but the size, cut and texture told him it was tuna.

He stayed low profile and went to several small places. Martinez was in a little bar on a side street close to the water. Clint called Valdez with the information, then went to sit on the rail next to him. He did a double-take and fell off the rail.

Clint said, "Surprise! I'll bet you never thought you see me face-to-face again.

"Might as well sit down again. You aren't going anywhere. We can have a little talk."

Martinez got up, looked uncertain, and started to sit. He suddenly reached behind his back and came out with a switchblade – and Clint had a Glock 90 pointed right between his eyes. He froze and Clint took the knife, then put it and the Glock back in his satchel.

"You're used to a wire. You're about one third as fast as you'd have to be. You're wondering if you could take me. Feel free to try, but you're a long way from the first who did.

"All I want from you is confirmation that your father is in charge, not someone else."

"My father's dead."

"Don't play games! You'll regret it!"

"I tell you anything and I die."

"That's the choice you made a long time ago. Don't whine about it now! Every one of you big bad hit men whine when it's your turn. You knew the rules before you started."

He stared at the ground.

"Well?"

"Are the police in Culantro under his thumb yet?"

"No. They never will be."

"Then I'll take my chances with them."

Clint shrugged. The police truck from Santa Catalina stopped in the road. Martinez sighed and went out to the truck. He climbed in back. Clint talked to the driver and the other two officers a moment, warning about the knife and saying that wouldn't be all he had. Don't take their eyes off him for a second.

They put Twist-Ties around his wrists and left. They would take him back to Santa Catalina and Valdez could pick him up in the morning. Clint went to bed after calling Tyna and talking for more than an hour. Nito and Nicole were hits in Soloy. They understood why they couldn't run around without an adult close by in a city like that.

Clint had gotten the tone that meant a call was coming in several times while speaking with Tyna. He looked at the ID number and didn't recognize it, so called. It was Sgt. Garcia, Santa Catalina police.

"Mr. Faraday? I have been trying to contact you. We were transporting a prisoner for you to Santa Catalina, a Sr. Martinez. He moved around the truck sometimes. He jumped out four kilometers before they reached here."

"He escaped?"

"No. They were traveling at eighty kilometers per hour. He did not survive striking the pavement at that velocity. I do not understand why he would do such a foolish thing."

"It's faster and far less painful than what he expected if he was delivered. Thanks for calling. If you haven't informed Valdez, I'll call him."

"He was informed immediately."

So. Now he had to meet Don Muerte face-to-face, not a pleasant thought. He wondered what would show in his character. He was a person whose son knew he would be tortured to death to save him from being exposed. He was a person who would kill his son to avoid exposure and who would torture that son to be sure he wasn't already exposed. He was a sadistic monster. There were too many of them about lately.

Clint considered, then went to bed. No sense in driving back to Culantro tonight. He was tired.

In the morning he drove back to Culantro. He would spend the day in Culantro and go back to Remedios to see if he could face a monster. He was forming a plan. He didn't kid himself about this kind of sick situation. It was hairy and it was damned dangerous. This was a person without normal emotions. He saw Magalita at Gala's and sat to ask her a few questions. She was depressed over Ricardo. She didn't understand why he had pretended to be her novio or what he wanted.

"He killed your mother and her two sisters. He would marry you. After the two year period he would inherit your land when he killed you."

"I do not want to believe that."

They talked awhile. Ricardo always said his father was dead. She didn't know the man he claimed was his father wasn't.

"I have to face the father. This was all his plan. You have to be careful. He may try something else as bad."

She shuddered.

Clint parked outside the brothel-bar-etc. and went inside. His subject was sitting at a side table with a pretty girl. Clint went up to him and said, "Don Carlos Flores? I'm Clint Faraday, as I'm sure you know."

Flores studied him a moment, then told the girl to leave. This was business. He waved to a chair across the table. Clint sat.

"The food is very good here, Mr. Faraday. Order what you like."

"Anything without thallium. The lasagna was good last night. I think I'll have the rib-eye. Medium."

Flores didn't react to the thallium reference. He said he preferred wine with meals, but Clint could order whatever he liked. Clint ordered red wine.

"So. To what do I owe the somewhat dubious honor of your presence here?"

"Bad luck, I suppose. You know that your son committed suicide last night rather than have to testify against you?"

"My son? I have no son."

"Oh, come on! That's a very damned hard thing

to miss! Ramón and Martinez were both your sons. You seem to use even your own sons as much as you can, then discard them like used snot rags."

"How do you mean, hard to miss?"

Clint held the shiny chrome napkin dispenser in front of his face. He shrugged.

"It's a dominant that neither of their supposed fathers carried. Ergo, they weren't the fathers. You carry it very plainly. I haven't seen anyone else in the area who has the feature."

"Please enlighten me as to what feature you refer?"

"Your ears."

"Ears? They're ears! Perhaps slightly smaller than many others, but ears."

"The lobes. They have a thickness pattern that looks like a cashew nut. It's a genetic dominant. It says something about other genetic traits.

"For instance: your father died before sixty of clogged arteries. Massive congestion of major arteries. His father probably did, too. You will."

He looked shocked. "I don't ... I didn't ... what is this? My grandfather was fifty two and my father was fifty six. I am fifty six. You are saying I will die soon?"

"Uh-huh. You have both circulatory and heart problems and tend to weight problems that you control with a lot of effort. Your cholesterol level is high, which is why you eat a lot of fish and chicken and never red meat. You control your weight, which is probably why you aren't already dead.

"That's beside the point. Murder is the point."

"You can't prove murder or even improperly crossing the street against me."

"Wha...? Er, is Dona there? And seis seis ocho quatro nueve dos uno cero. I was reading your number from the ledger in the corregidor's office. I can prove one hell of a lot more than jaywalking against you."

He looked thoughtful. "Well, be that as it may, shall we enjoy the food? I don't like this tension at mealtime. It disrupts the digestion."

It was a strange meal. Flores was the perfect host. He knew some interesting stories and some good bawdy jokes. They finished the meal and he asked if Clint was going to arrest him now.

"No. When I can tag you for the big one. I just wanted you to know where we stand and that no one else is to be harmed. You aren't getting the land and wouldn't live to get it if Ricardo married Magalita and waited the two years before that kind of inheritance law kicked in."

"Yes. Well, could you give me a reference to look up about the ear shape thing?"

"I read about it years ago, studying for a case. The victim died in that case unexpectedly at fifty nine years of age. A friend had seen the study and gave me a copy. I've seen two others with that dominant, one of whom is still alive, but only twenty four or five years old. The other died at fifty three.

"Google ears, heart, cholesterol or ear shape and congestive heart failure or whatever until you find it. I think it was a German group who made the study."

He nodded. "I will, most surely, be speaking with you again. I won't look forward to it, but there it is. I think you will not find proof of anything more than a small bit of bribery. That is an expected thing here."

"That's a sad fact, but I'll find more. I always do."

"Yes. I have seen that. It is what makes me wonder."

Clint drove back to Culantro for the night.

Had he accomplished anything with that bit? Flores was smug and thought he was above being prosecuted. He was now concerned about his heart problems. The added worry would tend to hasten his death from massive congestive heart failure. The study had shown that it was possible to delay death for many years if the diet was watched very carefully and cholesterol-lowering medicines were used when the patient started the treatment while still young. Flores was already fat, the major no-no. He was doomed.

What had led to Clint suspecting him in the first place was the dead aunts. He wanted their land. A map of the area showed that he could own the land all around the little town with that finca. He already held all the rest except the national land to the west, which he could buy from the government. It wasn't comarca. He would turn it into a little fiefdom.

Knowing Flores was behind it and that he'd caused the deaths of the aunts and the crooked cops and corregidor and not being able to prove it was pretty much what Flores was depending on. It was why the initial smugness. Now he was unsure, which would add to his tension.

The positive thing with this case was that it had exposed a couple of other little situations that could develop into much the same kind of thing. Valdez would suggest that every town be checked at rotation schedule points to be sure the ones not on the schedule were not on it because of their own choice. He would also suggest that every corregidor was investigated at rotation times for complaints filed against them. Clint knew from personal experience that a few of them were the lowest kind of corrupt thieves. The police would guarantee protection to all those who filed the informal complaints against any corregidors and would be guaranteed protection if they filed complaints against the police. The complaints would be investigated to determine if they were true, in which case charges would be formally filed against the corrupt officials.

The informal bit was because there would be a lot of charges that were no more than people getting pissed because they were stopped for a drunk check or something and their bribery didn't work. Clint had campaigned for all police officers to carry recorders to be used when any person was detained or questioned about anything. If there were complaints about shakedowns or such and the officer didn't have a recording to refute it, remember that you are guilty until proven innocent in Panamá. It's *prima facie* evidence of corruption to not use the required recorders.

Weird. Clint's mind went down strange paths when he was at a loss for what to do next.

Okay. The plan was to get all the land around the town and to set something up like a little personal kingdom. The Pacific ... he had an idea! He wanted to see if the government had been contacted about that land to the east. If Flores got his own added to that along the coast to the east he would have a place to bring in contraband. It could be brought directly to the town docks and the police would check every shipment that came in from anywhere to be sure it was legitimate.

That meant connections with someone running illegal cargo. Ninety percent of that would be drugs. Most were shipped on the Atlantic side to intermediate points like Panamá. Almost all the Pacific shipments went to Mexico or California. It wouldn't be watched closely for some time – time enough to make a few hundred million.

Was this Flores' deal or was he number two? Maybe number three?

One thing was certain. Clint Faraday might have solved the case of the dead aunts, but there was a hell of a lot more than that little bit. His puzzle was only a piece of a larger one.

How trite!

Clint went to the police station where Valdez was still going through all the records for the past four years, which is when it seemed to have started. He explained that people were being placed into minor positions who could influence who was placed into higher positions who could influence who got put into critical positions. Clint looked thoughtful, then said he had to know who was in contact with Don Muerte Flores four years ago, or maybe five.

"Flores is Don Muerte? I wondered. I have been checking on anyone the people refer to as 'Don' here. He and Milajuez are the only two. Ronaldo Milajuez is above suspicion. It was a tenuous suspicion, but a suspicion.

"So. What is it you're concerned about? You are acting strangely."

"Esteban, I need to know something about government land and how you buy it."

"Govern ... like the land east of here? Flores was trying to surround the town? Why?"

"I'm not sure, but I have suspicions of my own."

"You go to the catastro for information locally. It will be in Remedios. This is handled through David, which is handled through Santiago. If a large parcel is wanted it will most probably be handled in Santiago eventually, so any smart purchaser would go there."

Clint sighed and called Tyna to talk with her and the kids – and to tell her he had to go to Santiago.

Santiago was a long drive, but he got there after dark and stayed at the Hotel Bocas del Toro. In the morning he went to the catastro head offices and asked for information about anyone who wanted to buy large parcels of national land in Chirqui close to Veraguas. He was sent to an office that had all the records of applications anywhere in the country.

A search of more than half an hour came up with an application that was filed two years ago for the parcel in question. It was placed on hold for a corporation. The time of the hold was two years and was up in less than thirty days.

"I am acting for the Policía Nacionál," Clint said. He showed her the papers. "I must know who filed that application. It is evidence in three of the murders."

"Three of the murders? But ... how many were there?!"

"Seven or eight – that we know about."

She showed him the application form. It was to an S.A. corporation and was handled by a local attorney. He got a copy of the first page and went to the attorney's office. He sat for nearly an hour, then was escorted to F. D. Lange's office. Lange was a thin man in his forties with a permanent pious sneer on his face and a way of looking over his half-glasses at Clint that made him want to smack the sneer off his face. He made it perfectly clear that he wasn't giving Clint Faraday any information whatever about any case he may or may not be handling.

Clint said he only wanted the one name. That was not privileged information to the police.

"Then you will follow the legal procedures for obtaining such information?

"I have an appointment. You may go."

"Okay. Your call!"

Clint went outside where two patrol officers were just passing across the carretera on bicycles. He called them over and showed them the papers giving him authority. He said they were to go into that office, make everyone there leave, taking nothing with them. They would be allowed to return when Clint Faraday had served the court order allowing the police to go through their files.

Four minutes later Lange came screaming out of the fancy front door. He saw Clint standing there looking amused and demanded to know what was going on.

"I'm following proper legal procedure to obtain information that does not fall under privileged data. I can – and did – order everyone from the premises to guarantee you do not purge the information I seek. That order holds only until I bring the court order and conduct my search.

"I think just perhaps I'll wait until tomorrow before petitioning the court for the order. I'm dead tired from driving all the way here and going through the bureaucratic processes."

He'd wiped the sneer, the part that wasn't permanent, off the clown's face!

"I had hoped to finish this today so I could go back tonight, but that's the way things go when you have to work with lawyers. I'll see you sometime in the morning! I'll call your answering service when I have the order in hand and can meet you here. You can give me the information or I can take that office apart, page by page. Your choice!"

"Okay. You win. Having the police close the office will make the papers and TV and will hurt business."

"You're a lawyer! Yell police oppression, for the lord's sake! Make something that appears negative into something positive. Isn't that what you ... no, I guess lawyers make something positive into something negative."

"I already said you win. Call the officers off and I'll look up the information for you."

"Look up the information and I'll call the officers off."

A grin flashed on Lange's face. "Ah! You're educated in law, yourself!?

"Not lawyer law."

They went inside. Lange went to a file cabinet and dropped a file in front of Clint. Clint knew he would then yell that confidentiality laws were abused. Clint told him to simply write down the names of the corporation officers and he would be gone. He didn't ask to see anything further and didn't want it to ever appear that he exceeded his authority. That got another tiny grin. Lange wrote down four names and ID numbers and put the file back in the cabinet. Clint thanked him and left.

Clint checked out of the hotel and started the drive back to Culantro. He had a list:

Pres. Julio Cavano. Col.psprt number ********

V. Pres. Carlos Verano D. ced *******

Sec. Carlos Flores C. ced. *******

Treas. Mikail Vervnikov Arg psprt *********

Don Muerte was number three or four. He was taking orders, not giving them.

Or was he?

Clint drove into Culantro fairly late and went to the pensión to get some sleep. In the morning he went to the police station. Valdez was there to tell him a protest had been filed against him for breaching the confidentiality of a client of a law firm in Santiago. Clint grinned and dropped his Blackberry (which he only carried for this) on the desk. He set it to replay and the whole thing from when he went into the office was right there. No gaps.

He picked up the desk phone and punched Lange's number. When he answered Clint said the conversation was being recorded.

"You have filed a complaint against an officer operating from this station? Clinton Faraday?"

He disguised his voice, which was easy, because his voice was rather ordinary, anyhow.

"Yes. He came in here with his papers and demanded to see a file. He had closed the office and threatened to not allow me to reopen until he had the file in his hands."

"This is an official statement made after you have been informed the conversation is being recorded? What is your name and identification number, please?"

"Frederic Daniel Lange, cedula *********"

"Very well, Mr. Lange. You are aware as a lawyer, I am sure, that police officers on such assignments are carrying recording devices that are in use at all times."

"I ... er, uh!?"

"Would you care to rescind your statement or to change it in any way before this department jefe listens to Mr. Faraday's recording?"

"I, er, well, yes. I may have somewhat, er, misunderstood, er, or something. Perhaps I will rescind."

"Probably wisest. Making a false statement of case is perjury even by lawyers as of three years ago. Perjury can be a felony.

"Mr. Faraday is right here. He wishes to say something." Clint made a few noises and used his regular voice. "I sort of thought you would try to get back at me, but I thought you were smarter than that."

"It was mostly because of your advice that I did it. You said we lawyers could take something that is, in truth, negative, and make is seem positive. I was attempting to shift what my clients, in this case dangerous ones, would think of your having the information at all."

"Cavano is with a drug cartel?"

"No. Not him. He's in transportation, in a sense. The Russian is into something. I don't know what, but one does not, ever, question those people. They are dangerously insane.

"I have investigated a small bit about them, you see."

"He's Russian mafia in Argentina?"

"No comment! I have no personal knowledge of what he does in Argentina or elsewhere!"

"Understood. This conversation never took place. I'll erase it here, you erase it there."

They soon rang off. Clint raised an eyebrow at Valdez, who shrugged and picked up Clint's list.

"A reverse order of importance?"

Clint nodded. "I really think so. I really do!"

Clint thought, then called his friend in Isla San Cristóbal, Manny Matthews, who was actually Marko Bocinni, a big mafia don from California who was living there as a normal resident so he could raise his family not being ashamed of how Pops made his. He asked about the Russian mafia in Argentina.

"Same as here. Crazy as loons according to the way we think. Dangerous."

"Into drugs big time?"

"Mmm. Maybe transportation. They're more into arms there. Gimme a name."

"Mikail Vervnikov."

"Don't know. Ten minutes." He hung up and Clint waited until the return call.

"Transportation of whatever. Uses an offload/onload scheme that keeps those things running. Nobody knows his transfer points."

"Thanks, Manny. We may be able to close this transfer point before it opens. It would involve as much as making slaves of a whole town here."

"Sounds like them, but they usually are smarter than to try that kind of thing. See who else is in it. If there's something like that you can bet he's not PIC."

"What I'm doing now is trying to find out who really is PIC."

They chatted a bit, then Clint hung up to think. He was sure he'd heard or seen something that would at least make this part a lot easier. There was someone who said something back when this started. Who was it? What was it? It had faded away from his investigation.

Was that it?

"Esteban, you checked on all these people?"

"Everyone who came up, yes."

"What about that secretary at the corregidor's office? Bertina or something?"

He looked at his list. "Amanda Bertes Verde? She moved here six years ago and was working at the police station as a recording secretary. She ... I'll be damned! She recommended Ramón!

"Let's see. She also recommended Jimenez, then went to work as soon as he took office! She was so pathetic I didn't pay much attention to her. I will kick myself in the ass for years for that little piece of unprofessionalism!

"So! She was working with them from the first day she was here."

"I wonder. What do you have from before she came here?"

Valdez studied the papers, turning pages over and going back.

"Nothing. She came from Santiago. Let me check the old personnel records."

He spent fifteen minutes or so looking up her file.

"She was born in the canal zone. Her mother was Panamanian, her father was Russian. She was a good student and went to police academy, then was a legal secretary when she moved to Santiago to work in a law firm. Guess which one. She moved here. You know the rest."

"You know what I'm thinking?"

"Probably what I'm beginning to suspect. She disappeared from our minds professionally."

"Was she running things or just the coordinator and brains?

"Is she still in jail?"

"No. Her lawyer got her out in an hour. He posted a guarantee of ten thousand dollars."

"That won't be anything at all to them. It's just drinking money. She'll be gone."

"No. She's still at her apartment. She is being watched."

"Then she doesn't think we can figure this out. We have to set something up ... was her number on that ... no. She was there. It won't be on the list."

"She probably was the one who called Don Muerte all the time.

"Let's call on Flores, shall we? I think I can get something here, but we'll have to appear to be concentrating on Julio Cavano, the corporation president."

They drove out to the ranch house, a true mansion with gates and guards. When Clint told them his name they were passed through. Flores was waiting on the wide front terrace. He invited them to tea. Clint said he didn't drink tea much. He told the girl to bring coffee.

They chatted a few minutes. Valdez made a reference to Cavano a couple of times and Clint immediately changed the subject before anyone said or asked more about him. They mentioned everyone involved in the case except Bertes. Clint saw Flores reach under the edge of the table and a faint buzzer sounded. Flores said he had an important call, please excuse him. He went inside the house. Clint nodded very slightly and said they weren't making much progress. He thought maybe Flores had caught onto the fact they were using Cavano as a ruse. They had to get Flores to bring up Amanda Bertes soon or this wasn't going anywhere and they'd have to find another way to get her story confirmed or refuted. She wasn't as tough as she thought she was. The meeting in the morning would put her ass on the line. She'd cave.

Clint could see the table was bugged. Flores was listening to them.

Flores came out the door and they sat back to act like they had been idly chatting about the excellent landscaping or something. He said he was meeting with some people in a few minutes and would have to request that they excuse him. Perhaps they could come back later or in the morning tomorrow. Valdez said they'd covered most of it. They would call if there were any questions left unanswered.

"Your stopping comment about Cavano was a little obvious, Mr. Faraday. He's just the puppet president of a corporation. Really, he doesn't even know what's going on here except that it concerns a ... company in Colombia that he represents. He isn't even aware we are not going to be doing business with that company. They are in it because they wanted to finance a ... place to move their product. A bigger company feels they would be a distraction and will repay them for their investment and they then will no longer be concerned with the project. Perhaps the project will never happen now. Not with me. You have shown me my fate. I have checked the internet and learned much. Had we held the conversation we shared in Remedios ten years ago I might have taken the chance. The odds would have been far better. Now I have to concentrate on not spending the very little time I have left in jail."

Clint laughed. "I told Esteban you were smarter than that. We could have simply asked you."

He smirked. "We all have little games we play when direct action would suffice to advantage."

They stood and soon left.

"What will he do?" Valdez asked.

"It's hard to say. I don't really know. I just want this stopped. He knew it was doomed when we dumped his setup with the police and corregidor. I just still have to wonder if he's the head honcho or if darling Amanda is. If it's her, she'll try it again somewhere else."

"If it depends on corregidors and police, it will

fail."

"We can hope. Let's get back. I want to relax. I think I can go back tomorrow. I miss my family and we are *not* going to be able to prosecute on this one. I don't even have to arrange for him to leave the country. He's Panamanian. He's under death sentence anyhow. I doubt it will be long."

They went back to Culantro. Clint spent the rest of the day meeting with old friends and making new ones.

Clint was putting his things in the car. The sun was just up and it was a pleasant morning. His phone buzzed. Valdez. He answered.

"Clint? Our problems are now solved with what to do about those people in that scheme to take over the town. Can you come to Bertes' apartment?"

"Yes. I'm packed and can stop by on my way out." He remembered he didn't know where her apartment was and called back. It was just a few streets away. There was an ambulance standing at the entrance. They were loading someone into it. Valdez saw him drive up and pointed across the street and a little way farther ahead. There was a Mercedes sitting there that Clint had seen before.

"Flores?" he asked when he went to Valdez. "What happened? He went after Bertes?"

"Yes, it would seem. That's him being loaded into the ambulance. It seems he had a heart attack after killing her. Ricardo must have learned the method from him."

"Wire around the neck?"

Valdez nodded.

"Is there a Clint Faraday here?" the ambulance attendant asked. Clint said he was Faraday.

"Don Carlos wants to talk to you." He waved inside the ambulance.

Clint climbed in and asked, "She was the head of it?"

"Yes. It was an idea her father had invented, but he died before he could put it into use. She had added some things. None of us would survive after the plan was working. It's over.

"Clint, it was Ricardo acting under her orders with the women. I would buy them out at a high price. There is an unending supply of money in this kind of venture. Ricardo taught me the way to use the wire. He said it was a perfect method because it was fast and the victim couldn't even cry out.

"I have noted in the past month or so that my health is suffering. I am deteriorating rapidly. I have had two bouts where I was in great distress. I will not live another two months, I'm sure.

"You were here because of the three women. My

plan was for Ricardo to marry Magalita and talk her into selling. The others would do that because they would be secure and could move to a better place. Amanda thought that would be too slow. Ricardo did not really care for Magalita and didn't like her mother and aunts. They disdained him as the trash he was.

"I ordered the death of Ricardo. None of the others. He did not jump out of that truck. I ask that you not pursue that. The ones who did it had personal reasons. They were in early training in security together. He had stayed in the home of one just before he left training and had raped the man's mother and beaten his sister.

"That is in the past. Let it also die. There is no justice in making a person who has applied justice suffer for it."

Clint nodded. Flores suddenly gasped and his face contorted with pain. It passed.

"I think two days instead of two months in my life. Your friends near the town and a few in the town will be greatly surprised when I die. I am not quite the horrible monster you believed.

"I was. I have changed now that it is too late."

He jerked again. "Goodbye, my friend. I must get to the hospital. Not because I am dying, but because I cannot tolerate this pain."

Clint stepped out and said to take Flores to the

hospital. He told Valdez Flores wouldn't live more than a few days. Mark the case solved and closed. Valdez nodded. Clint shook his hand, got in his car, and headed for Soloy.

Clint roughed Nito up a bit and Nito laughed and hugged him. Nicole was with two of the local girls on the balcony, trading stories and giggling. Tyna brought everyone a guanabana chicha and sat cuddled close to Clint.

There was an "Oye!" call from the street and Nicole yelled to come on up. Rigo came into the room a minute later.

"I've finished my schooling and will be in Tula when the semester begins. I wanted to visit and to tell you of the good fortune of ten families."

"Yes. I heard that Flores left something for people he felt he had wronged or had caused to be wronged," Clint replied.

"He had several thousands of hectares around the town. It is divided among the thirty one members of the families who are still alive. I am now a land owner and Magali and the younger children are very rich. There is a new park near the sea for the town and a new wharf. There is a new part of the hospital where the best students from the medical universities will come to make investigations into genetic research and heart disease. Little Culantro is soon to become a major medical investigation center!

"There are strong restrictions as to the number of people who may come. The town is never to become a city with noise and pollution and crime. It is to remain very quiet and tranquil so that students and practitioners and scientists are not disturbed in their studies.

"He was a monster with a conscience at the end. He wrote a story about his life. He said that at the end he had a life of nothing but regrets. He had purged himself of the monster, but the regrets would follow him past the grave.

"It is sad that so many don't understand that. Regrets can follow you past the grave."

Clint nodded and sighed. "Care for some cold chicha? It's guanabana the way only Tyna can make it."

C. D. Moulton's works are available on most major outlets as printed or e-books. CD writes the CD Grimes, PI, mysteries, the Det. Lt. Nick Storie mysteries, the Clint Faraday mysteries, the Flight of the Maita science fiction series, books on orchid culture and many others of many types. Mystery, adventure, intrigue, science fiction, humor, fantasy, paranormal, mild erotica, and factual.

www.ingramcontent.com/pod-product-compliance
Lightning Source LLC
Chambersburg PA
CBHW072205150726
48002CB00014B/1340